© 2010 by Mike Reiss
Illustrations © 2010 by Johnny Yanok

All Rights reserved under the Pan-American
and International Copyright Conventions

Printed in China

*This book may not be reproduced in whole or in part, in any form or
by any means, electronic or mechanical, including photocopying,
recording, or by any information storage and retrieval system now known
or hereafter invented, without written permission from the publisher.*

9   8   7   6   5   4   3   2   1
Digit on the right indicates the number of this printing

Library of Congress Control Number: 2010926859

ISBN 978-0-7624-3524-1

Cover and interior design by Frances J. Soo Ping Chow
Edited by Jon Anderson
Typography: Archer, Metallophile, Oklahoma, and Swingdancer

Published by Running Press Kids, an imprint of
Running Press Book Publishers
2300 Chestnut Street
Philadelphia, PA 19103-4371

Visit us on the web!
www.runningpress.com

Just Too Cute

AND OTHER ADORABLE STORIES FOR HORRIBLE CHILDREN

BY MIKE REISS

ILLUSTRATED BY JOHNNY YANOK

RP | KIDS
PHILADELPHIA · LONDON

just TOO Cute

In New York,

in Central Park,

in the zoo,

in a cage,

was the **cutest little seal** you ever saw in your life.

He had big black eyes, and soft white fur,

and he was chubby from nose to tail.

People loved to watch the seal all day long.

"Oh look, he's eating a fish!" said a little boy.

"Oh look, he's playing with a ball!" said a little girl.

"Oh look, he's not doing anything!" said the mother.

"What a **cutesy-wutesy, itsy-bitsy, chubsy-wubsy**

little guy!" said the father.

ZOOM!

The zookeeper did not like animals at all. The lions were smelly and the monkeys were rude and the polar bear ate his favorite hat. But the zookeeper loved the little seal because he was just so cute.

One day, the zookeeper was feeding the seal a tuna sundae when he heard a loud commotion. An ostrich had gotten its head caught in an elephant's trunk and neither of them was very happy about it. The zookeeper ran off to help, leaving the seal's cage wide open.

And the little seal waddled away.

Now if people saw a tiger roaming free in Central Park, they would say, "Oh, help! A tiger! Save me!" But when people saw the seal, they just said, "What a *cutesy-wutesy, itsy-bitsy, chubsy-wubsy* little guy!"

The seal slipped and slid across Fifth Avenue. He did not wait for the light to change, and he didn't look both ways before crossing.

Because of him, a bus crashed into a taxi and a car smashed into a fire hydrant and a motorcycle knocked over a pretzel wagon.

Now if a person had caused all this trouble, the drivers would say, "Hey, buddy! Watch where you're going! I'm calling the police!" But when the drivers saw the seal, they just said, "What a *cutesy-wutesy, itsy-bitsy, chubsy-wubsy* little guy!"

The seal waddled up the street to a grand building. A sign outside read "MUSEUM OF ART." But the seal, who was not the best reader, thought the sign read "FISH MARKET." And so he went inside.

The seal went from room to room looking at paintings. Every time he saw one that had a fish in it, he ate it.

He ate twenty paintings in all, but none of them tasted very good. He knew he would never come back to this fish market.

Now if a guard saw a person eating the paintings, he would say, "Sir, there is no eating allowed in the museum. I'm afraid I must ask you to leave." But when the guard saw the seal, he just said, "What a *cutesy-wutesy, itsy-bitsy, chubsy-wubsy* little guy!"

The seal had never been away from his pool for so long, and he was getting quite hot. He stopped at a store called Tiffany's, whose windows were filled with diamonds. The seal thought the diamonds were ice, so he went inside.

The seal put on three diamond necklaces and two diamond earrings. He wore a diamond bracelet on each flipper, and a diamond wristwatch on his tail. He felt a little bit cooler, so he left the store.

Now if a customer walked out with all that jewelry, Mr. Tiffany would say, "You are wearing twenty million dollars in diamonds. You must pay for it, or I shall call the police." But when Mr. Tiffany saw the seal, he just said . . . well, you know what he said.

The zookeeper was worried sick about the missing seal. That night he got a call from the police. The seal was staying at the Plaza Hotel. He had checked in under the name "Mr. Bark."

The police found the seal in the fanciest room in the hotel. He was sitting in a gold bathtub filled with ice. He had ordered lobsters and crabs and oysters and shrimp cocktail from room service.

And he couldn't pay for any of it.

The police brought the seal to court. He was accused of many crimes, from jewel theft to jaywalking. Now if a person had broken all those laws, the judge would have said, "You're in a world of trouble, son." But when the judge saw the seal, he just said . . .

"You're in a world of trouble, son."

The people in the courtroom gasped. The zookeeper cried, "Your Honor! Can't you see how cute this seal is?" "Nope," said the judge. "I left my glasses on the bus."

The seal gulped.

The judge turned to the little seal. "Lots of folks come through my court every day. Some are beautiful, some are plain, and some look like Missouri mules," he said. "But I don't judge them by how they look. I judge them by the things they do."

"And so, I have two questions for you," said the judge. "First—did you know you were doing wrong?"

The seal nodded his head—yes.

"Second," said the judge, "are you sorry for what you did?"

The seal shook his head—no.

The people in the court were shocked. The judge had seen what they had not—that this was a very naughty seal indeed. And so the **cutesy-wutesy, itsy-bitsy, chubsy-wubsy** little guy went to jail . . .

. . . but it's the **cutest little jail** you ever saw in your life!

THE FRAGRANT SKUNKLING

Once there was a baby skunk
Like none the world has known.
Instead of spraying skunky funk
He squirted men's cologne.
He got a job at Bloomingdale's,
The fine department store.
So ends this sweetly scented tale
There isn't anymore.

THE OYSTER

What is moister
Than an oyster?
Grampa's Pamper
Can be damper.

THE PERFECT PET

Porcupines
Have pointy spines
Which makes it hard to hug them.
Killer bees
Are hard to please
And you don't want to bug them.
Jellyfish
Are smelly fish.

Electric eels can shock.
Bats have rabies.
Rats have babies.
The perfect pet's a rock.

the PENGUIN WHO BROKE the DRESS CODE

I'm **PETE THE PENGUIN.** For four weeks every year, my wife goes off to find food. I stay behind, standing on a block of ice, keeping our egg warm.

Oh, did I mention that ten thousand of my buddies do the same thing?

I spend a whole month, standing in the wind and the snow, staring at the backs of other penguins' heads. IT'S **BORING!**

One day, I asked myself, "What am I dressed up for? This is no party." The next morning, just for fun, I put on my red suit.

Then, from a far corner of the ice, I heard my pal Paul say, "Nice suit, Pete."
"Thanks, Paul," I said.

The next day, Paul put on a green suit.

"Lookin' good, Paul," I said.

"Feelin' good, Pete," he said.

The day after that, Patrick wore **PURPLE**, Pedro wore **PINK**, Puffy wore **PLUM**, and Paxton wore **PLAID**.

Within a week, there were penguins of every color out on the ice.
Call it **PENGUIN PEER PRESSURE**.

That's when I had a great idea. Keeping my egg between my feet, I waddled to the top of a hill. "Everybody listen to me!" I said.

"Paul, you stand over by Pablo. Peyton, you get between Pierre and Pavel. Pops, Pug, Pip, and Pepe—move a little to the left. Phil, stay right where you are."

"Perfect," I said.

We all took turns going to the top of the hill and barking out orders. We made all kinds of pictures: **PRETTY . . .**

PATRIOTIC . . .

POP . . .

PICASSO.

Those four weeks flew by in a hurry. We all had too much fun to be bored. And when our wives finally came home . . .

. . . We had a big surprise for them.

And we all had a surprise when the eggs started hatching!

Now the old ice floe is filled with happy families. And on Sundays, all the moms and dads go to the top of the hill . . .

. . . And watch the kids color.

ANiMAL POEMS for BEASTLY CHiLDREN

RABBITS, RABBITS, RABBITS

Father Rabbit married Mother

And they had a baby bunny.

And another and another.

So many it's not funny.

Soon there were a million bunnies.

They grew into rabbits,

Who had ten trillion zillion bunnies.

(They don't change their habits.)

Ten Little Dodos

Ten little dodos
Standing in a line.
One tried to ride the ceiling fan . . .
Then there were just nine.

Nine little dodos
Learning how to skate.
One thought he could outrace a bus . . .
Then there were just eight.

Eight little dodos left.
(Two had gone to heaven.)
One watched TV in the tub . . .
Then there were just seven.

Seven little dodos
Doing magic tricks.
One tried to saw his friend in half . . .
Then there were just six.
(Well, six and a half, really.)

Six little dodos
Were learning how to dive.
On the day they drained the pool . . .
Then there were just five.

Five little dodos

By the airplane door.

One stepped out to get some air . . .

Then there were just four.

Four little dodos

Perched up in a tree.

One forgot he couldn't fly . . .

Then there were just three.

Three little dodos

Visiting the zoo.

One pulled on the tiger's tail . . .

Then there were just two.

Two little dodos

Lazing in the sun.

One stayed out a bit too long . . .

Then there was just one.

One little dodo

Tried to be a hero.

He thought he could defuse a bomb . . .

Then there were just zero.

Now there are no dodos left

Because they wouldn't think.

If you do as dodos do

You might wind up extinct!

the APPALLING POLAR BEAR

Gavin Boloney was Hollywood's greatest animal agent. He would find talented animals and get them jobs performing in circuses. I'm sure you've heard of some of his clients: Russell the Crow, Jamie the Fox, Catherine Zebra-Jones, Tiger Woods, and Seal.

Gavin searched the world to find new animal actors.

In India, he found a snake that
could tie himself into any knot.

In Australia, a rabbit that could pull
a tiny magician out of a hat.

And in France, a snail that could
broil himself in garlic butter. Once.

One day, Gavin traveled to the Pole in search of a team of performing penguins. He was having no luck, probably because he was at the North Pole, and penguins live at the South Pole. About to give up, he suddenly crawled over a hill and saw a polar bear singing. But that wasn't all. He juggled clams. He did whale impressions. And he finished with a jazzy rendition of "Baby, It's Cold Outside". This bear was the greatest performer he'd ever seen.

OORK OORK OORK

"Polar bear, I'm going to make you a star!" Gavin said.

"Okay," said the bear.

Gavin booked the polar bear in Cirque de la Jerques, a fancy circus from Paris. Sure, it was Paris, Texas, but still it was classy. It cost eight dollars more than a regular circus, and the clowns acted like they were better than you.

The polar bear opened the show, singing a dozen songs in perfect
French. Then the dancers came out. They wore beautiful costumes that made
them look like cakes and pies and delicious French pastries.

And the bear just lost it. He ate every one of the dancers. Then he ate the acrobats (who objected loudly), the mimes (who didn't say a word), and the first three rows of the audience.

"Deee-licious," said the polar bear.

After the show, Gavin Boloney was very angry with the polar bear.

"I really shouldn't perform when I'm hungry," the bear explained.

Gavin said, "If I get you another job, you've got to promise me you won't eat everyone there."

"I promise," said the polar bear. "Cross my heart and hope to die."

The next job the polar bear got was with Ding-a-Ling Brothers Bumble and Bungle. This was a very cheap circus. The cotton candy was just cotton, and the peanuts were the Styrofoam kind that things come packed in. Instead of a Bearded Lady and a Fire Eater, this circus featured The Bearded Man and The Guy Who Eats Fairly Spicy Food.

The polar bear did a wonderful act, which was worth the price of admission (sixty-five cents). Then, the ringmaster came out to announce the next performer, Cupcake the Elephant. "Cupcake?" said the polar bear.

And the bear just lost it. He ate the elephant and the ringmaster and The Bearded Man, and The Guy Who Ate Fairly Spicy Food, and six clowns. "Deeee-licious," said the bear, even though the clowns tasted funny.

After the show, the polar bear shrugged, "I guess this is why you never see a polar bear in the circus."

Gavin Boloney was furious! "You promised you wouldn't eat another circus!" he cried. "Cross your heart and hope to die."

"I can't believe I said that," replied the polar bear. "I'm pretty sure I said 'Cross my fingers, hope to lie.'"

Now if you turn back to page forty-five, you'd see that's not what the polar bear said at all. But we should really keep moving forward.

No circus would ever hire the polar bear again. So his next job was at a birthday party for a pretty girl named Jemima. It was a wonderful party with volleyball, pony rides, and a petting zoo. The polar bear sang a few songs and told a few jokes, and was a perfect guest—until they brought out the birthday cake.

And the bear just lost it. He ate the birthday cake and the petting zoo and the pony. He ate all of the guests (which didn't bother Jemima much) and all of the birthday presents (which bothered her a lot).

"Deee-licious," said the bear, even though the birthday candles gave him heartburn.

Most people like happy endings, and so I've decided to give you one.

After the party, the bear apologized to Gavin Boloney. "I feel sick about

what happened," he said. "I mean, really, really sick. Sick to my stomach."

And with that, the polar bear threw up.

He threw up the circus dancers and the lion and the lion tamer and the clowns and the elephant and the pony and the petting zoo and every one of Jemima's presents. Everything was a little bit sticky, but none the worse for wear.

Then the polar bear put on a show for all the people and animals he had eaten. He tap danced and did card tricks and balanced a minivan on his nose. And everyone agreed it was worth getting eaten to see such a wonderful show.

So if you like happy endings, you can stop here. It's not what really happened, but it is happy.

Here's what really happened.

After the birthday party, Gavin Boloney went to meet with the polar bear. And if you guessed that at a meeting like this strong words would be exchanged, then things would get ugly, and someone would wind up eating someone else—you'd be right.

For, in the end, Gavin Boloney ate the polar bear.

"Deeee-licious," he said.